A Battleaxe and a Metal Arm 5:

The Wizard's Tower

Samuel Fleming

Copyright © 2021 by Samuel Fleming

Cover Art by David Leahey

ISBN-13: 978-1-954679-15-3 (paperback)
ISBN-13: 978-1-954679-14-6 (ebook)

Thank you to my Beta Readers

and to my First Reader,

Mel.

Contents

Previously… ....*vi*

The Staircase *1*

The Arboretum *11*

Ash and Frost.. *26*

The Obsidian Spire.. *36*

The Ramparts *48*

The Wizard's Sanctum... *57*

Spoiler-Free excerpt from BAMA 6............................*ii*

Thank you for Reading ....*iv*

Connect with the Author ....*ix*

"In spite of its inevitability, death is never easy, for it is a mortal's reckoning with an immortal state. All creatures fear death."
—undefined

Previously…

Helesys and Taunauk found themselves journeying deeper underground, beneath the oppressing shadow of the dungeon. They followed the hollow trail of the greatworm until they came to branching burrowed paths. There they were set upon by a giant lizard. Though they repelled the beast with axe and warding light, Taunauk's torch fell over the edge of a pit and down onto the sleeping greatworm. The pair were forced into the small caverns to escape the blue skinned worm. They crept carefully through the tunnels while watching for the stalking lizard. In one of the many paths, the lizard bolted and grabbed Helesys by the shoulder. It's speed was blur, but so was Taunauk's. The barbarian struck the lizard with Everfall and freed his comrade. Then Helesys blasted the lizard, crippling it. Taunauk's axe silenced it a moment later.

Further down, the rock of the cave gave way to brilliant resin, arranged in hexagonal shapes. Shortly after, they encountered the denizens of the Hive: Mindless drones, hulking guard bugs and scions—bugs with inherent magic that came from their flowing antennae. They bested a scion and a guard, then evaded more. They found Terran slaves—mind controlled and made into drones. Helesys and Taunauk followed the Terran drones to an egg chamber and then to the Queen's chamber.

The Queen was a towering giant who bade them to stay and help her hive dig. To help her escape the dungeon. Helesys threatened the Queen's egg sac with her wand arm and convinced the Queen to let them go. Helesys and Taunauk escaped deeper into the underground, heading toward what the Queen called "the Crystal Depths."

But the Queen had one final trick for them: The Spider King Paraxnae burrowed out from under her skin and then chased after them. Of all the beasts they had met in the Dungeon, Paraxnae's speed was horrifying. If not for her the weaver's hex and their combined might the Spider King would have torn them apart. In the end, they left the creature in a mangled heap. They did not kill it—dared not kill it and let it loose upon other realms. The drones carried away the king's crippled body and even then it stabbed and ate its own children.

Next, the weaver and barbarian came to an underground chasm and a hanging rock bridge. Down below was darkness and certain death. They watched as bug drones walked over and eerie, monstrous tentacles reached up from the depths to snag them and drag them down to whatever creature lurked below. Helesys and Taunauk crept out onto the bridge, ready—or so they thought. Their weapons tore and slashed through the first tentacles, but then the cavern shook and dozens rose in their place. As the cavern shook, the land bridge began to collapse. Helesys ran and leapt across the gap and was snatched.

With her wand-arm pinned, she flared her banishing light and burned both the creature and herself in the process, but it was enough to free her from its grasp. The weaver turned, called upon her arcane power and fired downward—not to hurt the beast below, but to send her body hurtling upward from the recoil. As her blast impacted the bottom and the creature, she glimpsed the gaping maw of criss-crossing teeth and hundreds of eyes, and then they vanished. Helesys reached the top of the momentum from her blast and turned in mid-air and fired again, this time the blast propelled her to the cavern entrance.

Though she had reached safety, Taunauk was surrounded on the last small portion of the bridge. The barbarian fought admirably but was trapped. With the last remnants of her strength, Helesys called for him and covered his inhuman leap across the immense chasm. Her blasts tore through rows of arms, protecting the barbarian as he soared. He nearly didn't make it, but clambered up the cliffside to safety. Once outside the chasm, the beast below retreated and left the two to rest a moment.

They pressed further, deeper, into the cavern and toward more light. The rock gave way to glass. There were creatures trapped just beneath the surface: Bugs, another terrible lizard, goblins and twisted half-men, half-animal creatures, and men made of steel and cable. Then they came to a blocked passage. Behind the thin wall of glass, Terran shapes glowed.

Helesys spoke to them and her gauntlet translated. They sought passage, but the glassmen offered them neither passage, nor help. They were as trapped as every other creature

Thrice Taunauk has glowed golden—once when fighting Zhug's metal men and once when fighting Paraxnae. The last was when speaking with the glassmen, though the barbarian could not remember what he said.

Ultimately, the glassmen granted them a swift death and sent Helesys and Taunauk back to the beginning, back to that stone room lined with sconces. In spite of their mounting questions, Helesys felt confident that one day she would pry the answers from the stones themselves.

~ ~ ~

The Staircase

The weaver and the barbarian stalked the long hallway and this time found no flooding, no wormsign, no forest. This time they found stairs.

The hallway opened up to a massive spiral stairwell. It was nearly fifty feet wide and thirty tall. Each step was nearly two feet high and the same wide, so large that neither Helesys nor Taunauk could take them in a single step. It was a place made for giants. The stone walls were lined with sconces and high above, tapestries hung depicting ancient battles. Every few tapestries were adorned with wolves. Helesys rubbed the edges of the wolf-plate tucked inside her robe.

Up or down? The stairwell seemed to beckon them in both directions. Helesys thought back to that first death, finding a branch in the hallway and not being able to travel both.

She snorted.

"What is it?" Taunauk asked.

"Up or down? It is a false choice. Both lead to death."

The outlander smirked. "Black humor. Back down to the depths?"

Helesys deepened her voice. "*I shall go first.*"

"Not on your life. Upwards then."

~

It was an easy decision to make. They stalked up the giant stairs—up for the first time. Taunauk led with shield and axe in hand. Helesys just behind with gauntlet humming quietly. She thought of reaching the top, to one of the jagged spires she had seen from the infinite wall. Maybe if they could reach the top of one of those, then she could see the terrible kingdom they were trapped in. Maybe she could even see over the infinite wall and see the limits of the world.

As the pair crept higher and higher, Helesys noticed the hallway was getting smaller. It was a slow process—the giant hallway might have only been a foot narrower each time, but after five rotations it was apparent.

Just when Helesys's legs warmed, they came to an alcove in the center of the stairs, cut into the support pillar in the center. She and Taunauk walked close to the alcove and peered around the corner.

Inside was a stone statue of a man and a stone lizard beside him. Of the two, the statue of the man looked older. It was pitted and cracked around the joints. In contrast, the lizard statue was thick limbed and immaculate—and breathing. Helesys stared at the pair of statues for what felt like a full minute to be sure: The lizard statue was not a statue. It was breathing perhaps twice a minute.

Helesys thought of the giant lizard from the tunnels between the greatworm borehole and the hive, and was thankful this one was smaller. This lizard might have stood as tall as her hip, rather than her shoulder as the giant one had.

Taunauk glanced back at her and gestured that they should continue upward. With any luck, they would pass by the sleeping lizard.

But as soon as Taunauk tried to climb one step higher than the alcove, the lizard snapped awake. It hissed in a long drawl.

Beside it, the stone man stirred. It lumbered forward, moving with the sound of scraping stone. The barbarian and weaver backed away, giving the statue and the lizard a wide berth. The stone man and lizard stopped just outside the alcove. The short-snouted reptile snapped at them, its back arching and tail coiling. It had nubs just behind its shoulders, as if wings were meant to grow there.

"You are not allowed here," the stone man said. It's voice was a mix of flesh and rock, of gravel being ground together.

Helesys looked to Taunauk, but his eyes were fixed on both. Her arm whirred with power and within it she felt the wordless whisper of the magekiller token. The language of dripping blood, stuttered step, of a gasp caught midway in the throat. She had felt the same power when under the spells of the druid wolf-mother and the scions of the hive—as if the magekiller token was hissing and warning her of magic.

"You are made-things," Helesys said with realization. The Deacon had used similar magic, but these were so very different from what he had made.

"You are not allowed here," the statue repeated.

Taunauk said, "They are guards. Simple things."

Helesys smiled, for the barbarian was as smart as he was formidable. "You are right. Stone man, can your master hear us?"

"You are not allowed here."

The weaver sighed. "'Tis a shame. We would rather talk."

"Come on then!" Taunauk slammed his axe against Everfall and growled.

The lizard jumped at Taunauk and as it flew through the air, the stone man breathed fire after it. The fire stream blossomed and seemed like it consumed the beast. Helesys leapt to the side, away from the blast. She felt the heat behind her, heard the slam of the lizard hitting Everfall, and the roar of flame and barbarian.

She regretted it immediately. The weaver landed hard on the stone stairs and rolled before catching herself in a crouch. Taunauk crouched behind his shield and backing away toward the wall, trying to shield himself against the stream of fire and the circling lizard.

Helesys raised her arm and fired a volley of blasts at the stone man. Purple energy slammed into him, stuttering its fire breath and nearly knocking it over. Chips of stone scattered against the stairs, but the stone man was only caught off guard for a moment. It turned and breathed fire toward Helesys.

The weaver fired again and again. The purple beams cut through the fire, splitting it so that she was spared the brunt of the heat, but still the fire came. Whatever magic bore it on was relentless, and she could no longer tell if her blasts were striking true.

As fire and arcane energy pushed against each other, a reptilian squeal was cut short. Then the fire listed as Taunauk charged the stone man and pinned it against the inner wall from behind. Fire charred the wall and finally ceased as it struggled to push away. Barbarian and magic construct strained against each other.

"Now! While it is—"

Helesys was already sprinting up the stairs toward them.

Though Taunauk had pinned the stone man from behind, its head turned with a slow, ominous scraping, turned and kept turning. The barbarian's eyes grew wide as the stone man nearly eye to eye with him and its mouth began to glow.

Helesys reached Taunauk and the stone man, ready with her gauntlet, vibrating with power. She placed a hand on the glowing mouth and released the pent up energy. The stone man's face exploded, as did several feet of the wall behind it. Taunauk released it and the stone man dropped to the stairs in a slump. Its arms and legs separated at the joints, becoming little more than a broken statue.

Both coughed from the cloud of pulverized stone that lingered in the air.

"That wasn't so bad," Helesys said.

Somewhere above, they heard the faint scraping of more stone. Much more stone.

"Do not give breath to fate," Taunauk replied.

~

The body of the lizard dissolved into ash, crumbling like the stone man had. No blood nor bile remained.

The word *drake* came back to her: A made-thing in the same form as a dragon, but smaller and lacking wings and firebreath. She found it interesting then that someone had gone to the trouble to make both the drakes and stone men, rather than combining the two. Perhaps there were limits to what the craftsman could do.

Or *rules*… There were always rules.

The barbarian and weaver pressed forward and were met with three more stone men. The stone men marched down the stairs, taking each step in sync. One to each side of the stairwell and one in the middle, so that Helesys could not catch more than one in a blast. They breathed spurts of acrid fire, their combined blast making a wall of stinging heat that pushed the elf and outlander back down the stairs.

Helesys shot blasts from her arm, but they rang hollow against the stone men—the energy dissipated by their own magical fire. She dug deeper with each blast, compounding the power of her gauntlet slowly. She had no desire to risk injury so early in their journey.

Nor did the weaver want to overplay her abilities. After the way Zhug had scryed on them in the barracks, she assumed they were being watched here as well. She would not give away all her tricks or her limits.

Three drakes peeked out from the flames like sharks from just beneath the water's surface. Unperturbed by the fire and heat—purposefully immune to it. The made-things were not so simple-minded that teamwork was above them.

The drakes leapt from the fire, two beasts trying to over-whelm Taunauk. He met one with a thunderous swing of Everfall that sent the lizard crashing against the stone. His axe crashed down into the shoulder of the second and it let out a shrill squeal.

Helesys saw movement from the side and was hit from be-hind. The third lizard had used the cover of fire to creep up the wall and ceiling and circle her. It pounced on her back and pinned her to the stairs. She covered her neck with her mun-dane arm and felt the drake bite, its needle-teeth raking her scalp and piercing the elven chainmail of her sleeve. The weight of the beast down on her back, her ribs pressed against the corner of the stairs, and felt like they might snap. She felt the heat and bitter smell of the stone men's fire growing hot-ter.

Her wand-arm was pinned down at her side in the crook of a stair. Helesys churned power, thinking that even if her arm was pinned, she could blast the stairs and the recoil would shove the beast off of her—

—but her gauntlet had other plans.

Her wand-arm bent backward at the elbow in a way that flesh and bone could not. For a second she worried about missing, but she felt the scaly shoulder of the drake and worried no more. Power exploded from her hand and Helesys felt the pressure on her back release. She pushed herself to her feet and saw the body of the drake—split clean in two from the close-up blast—already dissolving into ash.

Beside her, Taunauk sliced through the last drake. Then they backed away from the approaching stone men, who were now alternating their blasts of fire to make one continuous wall of heat.

"I can make it through," Taunauk said.

"No. Wait."

Helesys thought of her spells and searched her memory. Most would do no good against the stone men, but there was one: Helesys thought of the green knight of the forest and how she had negated the knight's speed and the spider king's speed.

There was more than just that single spell. Magic was creation but it was also negation. If those statues could make fire, then Helesys could negate it.

The words came from somewhere deep inside her, "*Calor residuam.*" Her wand glowed and she felt the magekiller token spark inside the metal.

The wall of fire stuttered and waned, and for the first time she saw the outlines of the stone men—no longer shielded by their magic fire. But the fire did not stop completely.

"Be ready, Taunauk."

Helesys raised her gauntlet and blasted. Even though her power was consumed by the counterspell, her blasts were no longer blocked by the fire. Helesys timed her shots for the gaps in the flame wall and now they struck true against the stone men.

The barbarian waited, half-crouched and ready to leap.

Then Helesys saw movement on the wall. Something had come from behind them and run up the outside wall of the stairwell. The shape was black and rippled like a ghost. It ran high along the wall, passing over and then dropping behind the flames.

As it dropped, Helesys saw the face of a Terran. A man.

The fire breath from the outside stone man stopped abruptly and Helesys saw the man standing over the crumbling body—a brilliant white dagger in hand.

Taunauk leapt a moment later through the gap in the flames. He crashed axe-first into the middle stone man, splitting it in two. Helesys turned her gauntlet on the last that hugged the inner wall, the repeated blasts easily striking through its muted flames and shattering it to pieces.

~

In the aftermath, Helesys and Taunauk turned to the newcomer. The man slipped the dagger back into a sheath, the action almost too quick for Helesys to see.

His eyes were a piercing blue and his skin was a tan as deep as Taunauk's and yet clearly he was no barbarian. His features were sharp, yet he was no elf. His cloak was night-black, frayed and dappled with gray, the way a shadow might dance. He held out his palms in an offering of peace and Helesys saw his hands were wrapped in black bandages.

And the man stunk awfully—like he had waded through sewage down below. Helesys's eyes watered and she kindled her wand arm for fortitude.

"Thank you," Taunauk said. The barbarian didn't look phased in the slightest by the smell.

"Think nothing of it." The rogue pointed up the stairs. "Mind if I join you?" He said the words with surprising casualness.

Helesys said, "Perhaps some introductions—"

A quake cut her short. The entire tower and dungeon shook, scattering dust and shards of stone down the stairs. Then a growl drifted up from below—so deep and long Helesys thought it was another quake.

Thundering steps replaced the growl.

"Introductions can wait," the newcomer said.

The weaver and barbarian shared a glance, and the three of them jogged up the stairs.

Helesys knew she was a soldier. She was accustomed to hard exercise such as this and rarely got out of breath during skirmishes, but she had to burn her wand-arm to keep up with Taunauk and their new arrival. The arcane energy flowed through her muscles, giving her strength and endurance beyond the limits of her flesh. Even still, she could barely keep up with them. Taunauk bounded up the stairs like a jungle cat while the other ran as if he was light as the wind.

They hugged the inner wall as they ran. All the while, the thundering steps became sporadic and quicker. Whatever lumbered after them was gaining.

With each revolution the stairs narrowed slightly until it was less than five feet wide and they were forced single file.

From somewhere below, the creature screamed and shook the stairs. Its steps slowed and the walls shook viciously.

The newcomer paused on the stairs. "I think we're safe now. It's stuck."

The walls rumbled again, but no more footsteps sounded.

"What was that?" Helesys asked, heart racing. At least Taunauk was breathing heavily; the newcomer didn't seem phased at all by the exertion.

The cloaked man shook his head. He paced idly and for a moment lost the airy attitude he'd carried with him. "It's… It's why I smell this way." He shivered from the recollection.

Helesys fumbled for words. "The smell is not that bad."

"It's horrible," Taunauk said straight-faced, without even a wrinkle of his nose or a twitch in his eyes.

The rogue replied, "I honestly don't know how you both are standing it." Then he turned and walked upward. "It was bloody horrible. Horrible, I tell you."

Helesys and Taunauk followed wearily, leaving the mystery behind.

The walls rumbled one last time with muted protest.

~

They climbed one more turn of stairs before they ended. In the narrow hallway, the newcomer stood between Helesys and Taunauk. The only way forward was through a wrought iron door. Patterns of wolf's heads adorned the metal as they had the tapestries in the lower stairwell—as they had in other realms of the dungeon. To Helesys, they had become a constant reminder of their goal and of their imprisonment.

Except that this time, there was an octagonal space below the wolf's head. About an inch deep, with a geometric pattern cut into it.

Helesys smirked. She slipped the wolf-plate from her robe and handed the shiny octagonal plate to the newcomer.

"Now where did you get that?" the rogue asked, turning it over in his hands before passing it to the barbarian.

The weaver shrugged. "From a trapped water elemental back in the flooded temple."

Taunauk said to Helesys, "You were right about it being a key."

"Curious that you should stumble upon just the right door..." the newcomer added. "What do you think that means?"

The group ignored the question and watched with bated breath. Taunauk pushed the wolf-plate into the opening and the metal slid perfectly into the iron door. When it was pushed all the way in, hidden gears clicked and clanked with arcane regularity, like the ticking of some ancient clock.

The outlander reached for the door.

"Wait," the newcomer said. "Now that we have a moment for introductions, my name is Shawn."

Helesys pondered the odd name, but she had no more reference than a gut feeling. Both her and Taunauk gave theirs in return.

"You're the first I've met that are trying to get out of here. No one else trying to escape," Shawn said.

"Only those few in deaths," Taunauk replied. "Four for us."

"Seven here."

Helesys asked, "Where did you come from?"

"From below. Through the dead library, the fake treasure room and the muck-farming giant's house. Oh—you meant outside this place. ...I'm not sure. Have your memories come back?"

"They come in glimpses," Helesys said, ignoring the faint stench and trying to stay on topic. "Pictures and feelings."

Shawn echoed her statement. "I remember little and what I see is contradictory. I see glimpses of noble houses and glimpses of dirty city streets. I see the sun rising in both places, as if I've spent nights in comfort and in squalor." He glanced at each of their faces, waiting for them to share.

Taunauk stared off at the stone of the hallway—through it—recounting his memories like a quiet prayer. "I remember the open plains, hunting and trapping. I remember a life of solitude. Fainter memories of a tribe."

"You have that look about you," Shawn said as he looked the barbarian over. "Furs, hands, *axe*..."

Taunauk eyed him curiously. Cautiously.

"I mean nothing by it." Shawn stammered.

The outlander shrugged. "You are not wrong." He turned toward Helesys.

Helesys regarded Shawn with curiosity as they spoke, but it was nothing about *him* that tugged at her. It was *the feeling*. She remembered first seeing Taunauk and knowing that he was not a threat. Even coming to realize that there was a reason her and the outlander reappeared next to each other time and time again. As they'd wandered the dungeon realms, she recognized that feeling was more than simple non-threatening judgement—it was a kinship of a kind she did not fully understand.

That was the same feeling that tugged at her now—a flicker of recognition.

So when Shawn turned to her, Helesys couldn't help but ask, "Do we know you?"

"I'm not sure, but I hope not," Shawn said with a melancholy smile.

It seemed a ridiculous reply, so much that Helesys nearly laughed. "Why not?"

"Because we have not seen each other until now. If we die, I might not see you both again."

The weaver was left with pause. He was right. But then how could she reappear with Taunauk each time—an ally she presumably knew from the outside world? How could she feel the same flicker of recognition with Shawn and not be tethered to him as she was tethered to the outlander?

She couldn't give voice to the questions, nor did she want to waste the time to do so.

Shawn swept a hand past Taunauk and toward the iron door. "After you, big guy."

~ ~ ~

The Arboretum

The iron door opened up to a forest and for a moment Helesys feared that somehow they'd been transported outside. That they were in the forest, surrounded by the infinite wall.

But this forest was not the same. Here there were all manner of shrubs and flowering plants. Fine trimmed grass covered the ground in between. The air was humid and heavy… Almost inviting compared to the frigid forest of the wode. There were trees, but they only reached up fifty feet— not to the impossible heights of the trees of the wode either. Above the tops of the trees, was a glass and metal ceiling. Faint pinpricks of starlight showed through the glass…

Helesys thought eyes must have deceived her, for it was bright as day within the confines of the greenhouse. Her figure even cast a small shadow beneath her, as if a sun was directly overhead. She looked around but could not find a sun nor any other source of light, and the stars outside the glass were not bright enough to account for it.

"Some kind of greenhouse," Helesys muttered. "I wouldn't have expected that."

"Agreed," Taunauk said in return.

Shawn said. "I don't know; not much in here surprises me anymore."

They crept out into the greenhouse in a mix of caution and awe. Each took turns looking up and down, side to side, trying to gather a sense of the place.

There was a sharp, metallic clank behind them. Helesys whipped around, heart pounding and gauntlet whirring. Taunauk and Shawn turned too, axe leveled, dagger unsheathed.

There was nothing but glass behind them, glass panes that rose up to the ceiling and stretched across past the limits of her sight, to the distant edges of treeline—the door was gone—vanished when it shut behind them. Helesys ran her metal hand over the surface, searching for a hidden seam or illusory magic, but felt nothing but the smooth, cold glass.

"*Stercus*," she cursed. "There's nothing. The door is gone—along with the wolf-plate."

"Shit," Shawn said, reflecting her disbelief.

"I thought you didn't want to go back down?" She said half joking, half prodding.

"I would've liked the option." he mumbled.

Taunauk shrugged. "It changes nothing. Come. Let's see what danger awaits us."

Shawn took quick glances at the two. "Are you always so eager? ...Is he always so eager?"

Helesys calmed the churning in her wand-arm to a quiet thrum and wiped the beading sweat on her brow. "Look at it this way: We woke up from death, now we're on the 'fight things' part. We will either escape or we will die. If we fail, we wake up somewhere new. Repeat until we escape."

"Wake up. Kill stuff. Die. Repeat?"

The weaver nodded thoughtfully. "That is more succinct."

~

The greenhouse stretched on—further than Helesys thought possible. It was like the hallway or the infinite wall in that respect. And it was home to wonders the likes of which Helesys had never seen—or could not remember seeing.

There were walking-trees; great lumbering things with the bark-faces and beards made of vines that wrapped around their limbs and legs. They spoke with crackling voices, like the sounds of tree branches snapping. Tiny shrubs scurried like trained pets, weaving between their masters' steps. The arbormen paid the adventurers no mind, and in turn they gave the arbormen a wide berth.

Later in the distance, they saw a six-legged, golden deer that towered the same height as the arbormen. Its antlers were as wide as their branches. It walked softly in spite of its massive bulk. Long vines with golden leaves trailed from its antlers and gripped the ground. As it walked, the vines broke free and turned to water and splashed when they fell. Then new vines grew in its place. The grass was golden beneath its feet, as if each step created a glistening puddle of golden dew.

Helesys, Taunauk and Shawn stopped to watch the strange sight, all seemingly aware that they were in the presence of a forest god—one trapped like all the other manner of beings.

The god turned to them, staring with deep black eyes—stared for only a moment before the golden color began to fade; the grass turned green and the new color crept up the deer, replacing the brilliant golden fur. The green covered the god up to its snout and face and then its antlers. In the antlers, the trail of receding gold began to burn brilliantly, like lightning caught within. The vines were last, and when the Green had reached all the way through the vines and to the ground, the forest god vanished in a brilliant—silent—flash of autumn.

The three of them stood still and silent, staring at where the god had been. It was a sight and a moment that Helesys would not soon forget. One that humbled even Shawn to silence.

When they began walking again, they passed a pile of bricks—which might have been the remnants of a long forgotten chimney. Helesys thought of the Deacon of the forest village and his words that in time all things decay. In time, the dungeon would grind all of them to dust: Mortals and gods, alike.

Sometime later, they came upon a waterfall. Hearing it first, Shawn hastened his steps, and Helesys and Taunauk followed. The sound grew to a roar before they found it. It fell from a crack in the glass above and pooled in a small oasis. The flow was so thick compared to the small pool that Helesys thought that it must seep down through a crack in the ground, feeding some other part of the dungeon. Helesys and the others stopped beside the waters to admire the flowering plants that littered the area—a small reprieve.

Suddenly, Shawn jumped into the water, and both Helesys and Taunauk shied away from the splash.

"*Yes*. There is some mercy to be found here," Shawn said, wiping his eyes. The rogue waded up to the edge and sauntered out of the pool. He sat, slid off each of his boots and tipped out the water. Next he peeled off his socks and rang out dingy yellow water. "I'll take the chafing over the stench."

Helesys jested, "Got too friendly with a muck farming giant?"

"And his cow-demon. She had a long neck and these eyes, I tell you." The barefoot rogue mimed shooting rays from his eyes.

Shawn stood up and strolled up to a bunch of flowers, admiring the brilliant yellows and purples. "Now these are much too pretty a sight to be trapped here."

Helesys regarded Shawn and found herself smiling. She thought it was fitting that of the three of them, he was the first to talk after the things they had seen in the greenhouse. It was a ridiculous sentiment, for she did not know Shawn. ...Or did she?

Taunauk put the pommel of his axe on the ground and rested his hands on the top of it. "Do not admire them closely. The prettier the flower, the more dangerous it is."

"Nothing for your enemies to worry about then, eh?" Shawn retorted, a playful look on his face.

"Small things feel the need to be pretty. Large things do not."

Helesys smiled and pointed toward one of the arbormen walking in the distance. "I believe that walking-tree has flowers in its beard."

Taunauk looked to it, then shrugged. "It is a small tree."

With that, Shawn gathered his boots and socks. Helesys pulled out her canteen, giving the other two silent direction to do the same. They made sure to do so upstream of Shawn's entrypoint. The three filled their canteens, ready to continue on.

~

The greenhouse went on, much further than Helesys would've thought possible. Helesys wondered if it could be as large as the forest outside, but she would not tempt fate in such a manner. Knowing this is an impossible place made everything in her imagination seem possible.

They walked in a loose circle. Taunauk always in front, Helesys and Shawn content to follow on either side.

"Are we lost?" Shawn asked. "Tell me we're not lost."

Taunauk grunted. "We are not. I know the way back."

"But *where* are we going?"

The barbarian didn't reply.

Helesys pondered a moment and began to feel *something* in her gauntlet. A pull or a guidance... She pointed with her metal-arm, off toward rolling hills and treeless, open space—more or less in their direction of travel. "I feel we are supposed to go this way."

Taunauk seemed satisfied with her lack of explanation. Meanwhile, Shawn just stared at the pointed fingertips.

"I've got to get me one of those."

Helesys looked at him quizzically.

"Your arm. That is a strange contraption."

"Who's to say it is not merely armor?" she asked.

The rogue shook his head. "I very much doubt it. It looks far too graceful and twice you touched the grass and trees as if you can feel through it. Is it telling you which way to go now?"

Helesys smirked. "Not in such crude terms. It does not speak, but it seems to have instinct about direction and danger."

They walked on and the forest broke, giving way to rolling green hills, and when they came to the crest of the first, all three stopped in awe. The plains sprawled out before them, seemingly for miles. Another faint treeline was visible on the horizon. The smell of earth and grass floated on the wind. For a moment, it felt as if they were alone amongst the grandeur.

"What's wrong with him?" Shawn asked, nodding in Taunauk's direction.

Helesys turned and saw Taunauk looking out of the hills with watery eyes. He stood stiff with his axe clutched close to his chest. He whispered to himself, "*The blade holds the warrior as much as he holds the blade.*"

She had heard that prayer before… Back in the forest, the barbarian told her of home, that he was born on the plains. He also said that he was an outcast. That his family name, Aonar, was not a name so much as a title. It meant *alone* in the outlander tongue.

She could not tell what manner of emotion swelled in her steadfast comrade, but she felt compelled to answer Shawn. "The fields remind him of home." Though she omitted much, Shawn nodded and took the meaning—or enough of it.

"It is only a shadow," Taunauk said, lip quivering where voice did not. "Ours was an ocean of green without a tree in sight."

"One day," Helesys added quietly, leaving the rest of the promise unspoken. When that did not move Taunauk, she took a step forward.

The barbarian snapped from his trance and led them across the plains.

~

Sometime later, something in the sky above caught Helesys's eye. Not in the light of the greenhouse, but up above, in the night sky. Something had blotted out the stars as it passed overhead. Something big and winged.

It caught the eye of all three of them.

"Good thing we're in here," Shawn mumbled.

"Do not give breath to fate," Taunauk replied.

They crested the next hill and saw disturbed dirt. Huge mounds and heaps that twisted and turned. Littering the valleys between the hills. *Tunnels*, Helesys thought—each bigger than they were.

"Is that what you're talking about?" Shawn asked

Taunauk nodded reluctantly.

"Should we go around?" Helesys asked.

The barbarian looked over the hills and valleys, but shook his head. "Whatever creature made those has an equally large range. Keep to the hills where we can."

Taunauk drew Everfall and axe. Shawn drew twin daggers; one obsidian and jagged, the other a brilliant turquoise. Helesys merely let the power of her wand smolder.

They followed the barbarian as he threaded through the giant mounds of dirt. Now that they were between them, the size was daunting. Each was wider than Helesys's arm span and nearly as tall as her.

"Whatever creature made these," Shawn said, "hopefully they are long gone. Or sleeping."

Taunauk sighed.

They crossed the first hill and into the second valley when the ground began to rumble. The three adventurers stopped and turned to the direction of the rumble, weapons ready.

At first, Helesys feared they wouldn't see the approaching creature until it was too late. But the ground rippled and tore violently, slinging dirt and mud dozens of feet into the air. The loose dirt of still mounds blew apart as a creature burrowed through the earth, directly toward them. A roar sounded through the ground, a mix of a quake and a giant steaming kettle.

But more than the sound was the speed. Something bore through the ground—tore through it—as quick as other creatures might run.

"Run!" Taunauk yelled. Helesys ran to the right, Shawn to the left.

The roar grew deafening as the monster broke the surface. Helesys turned and saw Taunauk charging to meet the creature. A pale monster erupted from the ground, pale, slick and smeared with dirt and clay. It was bulky and its body was segmented like armor plating. It yawned and plate after plate slid back, revealing a mouth full of spiked teeth nearly tall enough to swallow the barbarian whole.

Taunauk rolled at the last moment, avoiding its maw and slashing across its armored hide. His axe bounced feebly off.

Helesys was ready as well, and when the monster passed Taunauk, she leveled her gauntlet and fired a blast at its side. The purple burst around the dense plates, rolling off harmlessly. She watched as the beast dove headfirst into the ground. Then disappeared down into it as swiftly as it came, propelled by short legs and a powerful tale.

"More are coming," the barbarian growled.

Helesys felt the tremors coming from her side and turned to find two more creatures charging, throwing up massive wakes of earth. "*Stercus.*"

On a whim, Helesys fired a blast at the ground a dozen feet away. She hoped the creatures would follow the tremor, but neither did. She shot four more quick blasts in the same area. This time both of the creatures turned toward the impacts. Helesys watched with satisfaction as her ploy worked, and both monsters burst from the ground to find empty air waiting for them.

The weaver turned toward Taunauk and fired four more quick blasts to the side of her comrade. When the gaping maw burst forth, Taunauk was safe and ready. He swung wildly, but again his axe bounced off the thick plates of the beast. It disappeared into the ground before Taunauk could swing again.

"Cursed *siorc talmhainn*!" the barbarian shouted.

"What does that mean?" Shawn called.

"Landshark!"

The pair circled round for Helesys and again she blasted the ground to the side of her. This time, the beasts were not dissuaded and charged straight for her. The weaver churned the power of her arm, calling on it not for a blast, but to bolster her strength. The power that churned within the metal flowed into her muscles, bolstering them, and when the beasts came, she was no longer scared.

When the sharks burst through the ground, she rolled out of the way easily and bounced to her feet. She smirked—her frustration momentarily overcome as she relished having a barbarian's strength and also because she had seen the underside of the shark. The armor was thin on their belly and slightly thinner around their tails.

"Taunauk, you must strike them from below!"

"*That is a fine idea.*"

Helesys minded his sarcasm as the great beasts disappeared below ground again. The beasts were smart enough to change their tactics, which meant they were smart enough to be baited.

The weaver kept her strength bolstered and when the sharks came round, she leapt straight up and over their waiting maws. Her stomach turned as she reached the crest of the new-found height. She watched the beady eyes of the sharks glance up at their prey before disappearing again.

Helesys landed and ran toward Taunauk, counting on the beasts to follow. They did. Now all three sharks converged on Helesys and Taunauk.

"Be ready," she said.

Taunauk whispered, "*Freumhaichean de fiodha iarainn*," and she recognized it as the rooting spell. The same rooting spell that the green knight used to stand against the barbarian.

The first shark broke through, leaping nearly vertical in anticipation of its prey. Helesys burned power and rolled clear instead. Behind her, she heard the slice of Taunauk's axe and a bellow of an injured shark.

But the other of the pair came directly for Helesys, having sensed her roll across the ground. She dodged again, clearing its maw as it exploded from the ground. This time she charged her arm, compounded it, and fired at its tail. The blast penetrated the thin armor, and the beast roared as it dove underground.

She felt the recoil in her shoulder. With any luck, the pain would give the beast pause.

The weaver turned in time to see the first shark laying on its side, Taunauk silhouetted in front of it.

The third shark charged him and rammed him with mouth closed. The massive beast crashed head first into Everfall and a barbarian strengthened by magic. Taunauk roared, and the crack of bone plate against unyielding ironwood echoed through the hills of the greenhouse. The outlander stood tall behind his shield, unmoved against the massive beast. Snaps echoed through the beast as other plates cracked under the force of the sudden stop.

The ground beneath them was stained red from the seeping wound of the first. The tails of both landsharks thrashed. One in pain, the other in anger. They crashed against Everfall, bone plate again cracking against ironwood, but Taunauk stood firm.

The stunned beast turned from its immovable enemy and saw Shawn for the first time. The rogue stood some distance away, wide-eyed, but with daggers ready. Somehow, he had stayed still and avoided the entirety of the fray.

But now the shark charged Shawn. It roared through the earth—not content with diving under—but burrowing through the surface. Earth split and chunks flung across the hillside. Its tail was a blur of bone plate and mud as it propelled the beast.

Shawn didn't move.

Helesys fired, trying repeatedly to strike the shark's tail. Blasts struck, but the wake of churning dirt dissipated the blasts and still the beast charged.

Shawn stayed still until Helesys was certain the shark would run the poor man through. Then he disappeared behind the wall of dirt and bone.

And reappeared on the back of the shark, materializing out of thin air. Helesys saw only glimpses of him, but he was stabbing the beast with his two daggers. Seconds later, Shawn leapt off the beast and onto the ground. He stayed in a crouch, unmoving again.

The beast slowed, quieted, and finally dove underground. Shawn sheathed his daggers and sauntered over to the group.

Helesys turned her attention back to Taunauk and the wounded shark. The ground around them was uprooted with the paths of the beasts. The second shark had disappeared somewhere deep underground—its track no longer visible.

Taunauk stowed Everfall on his back and said a quick prayer. Then, with one decisive slash, he rended the underside of the dying beast. The pitiful gasps faded and finally ended.

~

The smell of earth hung heavy in the air. Helesys shook out the tenderness of her shoulder. She and Taunauk turned to Shawn, who looked immaculate in contrast to them.

"That was some trick," she said. "Teleportation?"

Shawn shrugged. "Simple misdirection. Appearing to be somewhere that I am not."

She asked, "And avoiding the landshark's ire while we fought?"

"Standing still and not making tremors." Shawn asked, "What about you two? It appears we're quite the capable team."

"Presumptuous…" she replied.

Again, Helesys felt the pang of familiarity and it stopped her short. There was something in his candidness. In his smile. It was something that she couldn't help but reflect. She looked to Taunauk and saw a faint smile on his face as well.

"I'm a complicated man," Shawn said. "Presumptuous is just a piece."

Taunauk turned and had walked around the dead landshark, examining it. A few moments later, he walked back around, rubbing his fingers together. "There is ash between the plates…"

He walked off toward the top of the nearest hill. Helesys and Shawn shrugged and followed.

The three of them looked out past the churned earth of their battle and out over the rolling plains, but saw nothing.

Behind them the bodies of the sharks were dissolving into dust and scattering on the wind.

"What are you looking for?" Helesys asked. "Scorched forest or fields?"

Taunauk said, "I'm not sure…"

"Perhaps if we could look out from a treetop," Shawn said. "But they're all the way over there."

"We don't need trees," Helesys said in slow realization. "Taunauk, give me a boost. I'll jump off your back." She stepped back half a dozen paces.

Thankfully, Taunauk understood, for if she waited any longer she might've lost her nerve. He leaned over, Everfall sitting squarely on his back.

Helesys flared her wand-arm and power flowed into her body. She ran and jumped onto the shield. Then Taunauk pushed up and Helesys leapt. A barbarian's strength bolstering her own magic-enhanced jump.

The weaver soared skyward, mouth open in surprise and in laughter. Up and up, higher even than the treetops.

She looked out over the greenhouse. The glass encompassed the limits of the domain. Over the plains, over the trees, and saw the limits of the space. Across the plains there was a black tower, one that nearly blended in with the night sky that lay beyond the glass—one that they might not have seen until they stumbled upon it.

Nearly at the apex, she turned and looked across the plains and saw that most of the greenhouse was indistinguishable from the rest. Except that a few hills away, she saw scorched hills. In the center of the black swathe she saw frost blue, and in the center of that, a small but incredibly bright blue light.

Then Helesys was falling—the sensation startling her—bringing her back to the room. She looked down and thankfully saw green grass and her comrades backing away. The weaver fell and hit the ground in a roll, her magic-enhanced body easily handling the stress.

She grinned ear to ear. "I see our destination."

~ ~ ~

Ash and Frost

They came to a clearing within a clearing. The grass was charred and ash clung to their boots. The smell of it hung heavy in the air as they walked through the black. Whole hills were barren; even the wind was dead.

"We're going in there?" Shawn asked. He had drawn the end of his cloak up in arm so it didn't drag through the ash.

"Yes. Follow me." This time, Helesys led the group.

Taunauk paused on every hill to stoop and check the ash.

"Copper for your thoughts," the weaver finally said.

Taunauk rubbed ash between his fingers. "Green does not burn easily. Not natural."

Helesys pointed across the next hill. There lay the center—the frost that Helesys had seen from above. And in the center *something* glowed bright. Like a star brought down from the sky.

"I've been thinking," Shawn said. "I do not think that all of these things are made-things. I think some have found a home here."

Helesys searched the newcomer's face and saw something between longing and sorrow or guilt. "What are you musing about?"

Shawn shrugged. "Just a thought."

Taunauk said, "If it is guilt you feel then it is misplaced. The landshark and the other felled beasts will find a new home somewhere else."

Shawn shook his head. "I do not think it is that simple. A home is a home and new ones are not so easy to find. But I agree with you big guy, that if they get in my way, I will not be the one to die."

They spoke no more of it and walked across to the frost covered hill. The change was sudden, both in the color of the ground and in the air. The ground was winter blue and Helesys saw her breath immediately after stepping onto the frost. There were even gusts of wind here where there had been none on the ashen hills.

"Sorcery," Taunauk said, breath steaming from his mouth.

Helesys could not tell if her comrade said the words with awe or disdain. He was unreadable as a mountain.

She turned and saw Shawn standing on the edge of the frost. "Come on. It's not that cold."

Shawn scrunched his face up at her, but stepped into the frost. He pulled his black cloak tight. "Movernus, it's cold."

"It is not far."

Helesys led them forward. There was ash beneath the frost and it left gray steps in their wake.

The effects grew stronger as they approached the source of the light and—Helesys suspected—the source of the winter magic. The wind rose to a roar laden with sleet. Frost grew thick and crunched beneath their steps. It was biting cold now and even kindling her wand-arm, Helesys knew she could not stay here for long.

Whatever sorcery this was, it was meant to keep others out. To keep them away from the source.

"Helesys!"

She barely heard Taunauk over the wind.

The weaver turned and saw Shawn doubled over in the out-lander's arms. His head and limbs hung limp. Taunauk's face and cloak were coated in frost.

"*Stercus.* Take him back!"

Taunauk nodded and waved for her to follow. Helesys shook her head and held up her gauntlet. Taunauk hoisted the limp rogue over his shoulder and trotted off, finally disappear-ing behind the swirling sleet. Leaving Helesys alone in the cold.

She turned and trudged the rest of the way to the light. The snow was so thick now that it was blinding and it came up nearly to her knees. She had only the pinprick beacon of light to guide her.

Two mounds appeared, and once she got close enough to touch them, she realized they were bodies. The first was almost completely covered in snow. Only its head and single arm were visible, the skin of both were thin and shriveled, wind-scoured—both the race and sex of them erased by the ele-ments. It looked as if it had been crawling on the ground. Crawling and reaching toward the second body with a frozen, outstretched arm.

The second body was kneeling, only its shoulders and head crested the snow. It's head was bowed, eyes closed in peace. Light showed bright from beneath the snow, a spot close to its chest.

Helesys scooped away snow with her metal hand to reveal the brilliant, glowing blue ring on the mage's hand. She reached down with both hands to slip the ring off the dead mage's fin-ger and found her mundane hand could barely stand to touch the corpse—only her metal hand could touch the ring. Helesys felt the icy, frost-laden surface with the mithril of her hand. She knew it was cold, yet it did not bother her gauntlet in the slightest.

It slipped easily over the shrunken knuckle, and when it was free the world darkened. The brilliant glow of the ring faded to a mundane crystal. The howling wind ceased, as did the snow. For a moment, Helesys thought she'd gone deaf.

"Helesys!" Taunauk shouted from atop the green.

Suddenly, the two bodies crumbled to dust in the snow without ceremony.

The weaver pocketed the magic ring and ran through the already melting snow toward her comrades, leaving the mystery of the dead mages along with all other crumbling things.

~

Helesys burned her arm and crossed the hills with superhuman speed.

Taunauk stood and held Shawn's limp body close, trying to warm him with his own heat. The poor rogue looked small in his arms. His head hung limp on the outlander's shoulder.

"Set him down."

Taunauk lowered him to the ground and the weaver minded his head. Kneeling beside him, she summoned her gauntlet again, this time summoning the warding light. Careful not to call upon its full power, lest it burn him, Helesys pressed it on Shawn's chest. It glowed and grew warm.

"Is he breathing?" Taunauk knelt beside them.

Helesys closed her eyes and focused on her hand. After a time she felt his chest rise, faint and very slow. She nodded.

"He spoke nonsense of floating on dreams—"

"—One thing at a time," the weaver said. She needed to concentrate. The weaver glanced at her comrade and saw the concern plainly on his face.

They stayed beside Shawn and watched as the color slowly came back to his face. Purple and blue gave way to faint red. His chest rose and fell, and finally his eyes fluttered open.

"I very much did not like that," Shawn mumbled. "Freezing to death is no way to go." He reached up with shaking hands and clutched her gauntlet. "That's a good trick to have."

Both Helesys and Taunauk smiled.

"You spoke nonsense," the barbarian said. "About floating on dreams, sculpting with sand, and kissing the feet of Preushom—"

"No. No." Shawn shook his head. Then sat up and folded his legs under him. The rogue pondered this a moment, then smiled. "Merely one of the symptoms of freezing, I'm afraid. The mind plays tricks on you. For some reason, I remember a story about a traveler that got caught in a blizzard. They found him naked and frozen the next day. Naked! So crazed, he thought himself warm, the poor sod. Do not believe my gibberish."

They pulled Shawn to his feet. Taunauk unclasped his cloak and wrapped it around their third comrade. The extra length pooled on the ground.

"It's a little big. But thank you."

"I'm sorry," Helesys began. Shame welled up in her at the turmoil she put him through. "I didn't think—"

"Think nothing of it. Was it worth it?"

Helesys pulled the crystal ring from her pocket. "I got it, if that's what you mean." She held it out to him.

"No, thank you. I've had enough of the cold."

"Even if it could protect against the cold?"

Shawn eyed the ring a moment, contemplating the idea, but shook his head wearily. "The things we draw power from also make us beholden to them. I suspect my blades have enough of my essence. Let's push forward. A walk will warm these cold bones.

~ ~ ~

The Obsidian Spire

They crossed the rest of the plains undisturbed, though they saw a great many things. They saw a migration of treemen and all manner of beast that followed. Shawn warmed up and returned to something akin to normal. He gave Taunauk back his cloak, and the barbarian seemed content to hide his massive shoulders beneath it again.

Again, the starlight beyond the glass walls flickered as a massive shadow circled far above the greenhouse.

All the while the black tower grew in their vision, blotting out the stars.

Helesys thought of when she and Taunauk had walked across the ancient forest and she had turned to see the dungeon—the castle—rising up to impossible heights. Its dark stone had done the same then.

"What do you suppose that is?" Shawn wondered.

"Our destination," the weaver replied. "It rises up beyond the greenhouse."

Then they were upon it. It was a sudden feeling—they crested one hill and the next the tower was close enough to touch. The void-black stone had played a trick of perspective on the mind.

The surface was sheer and impossibly smooth. At glancing angles, there appeared to be grooves of individual stones, but they disappeared when looked at directly.

The tower itself was much thinner than Helesys had supposed. It might have only been forty feet across when from a distance it had looked monstrous. Its height, however, was staggering and gave impossible, nauseating dimensions to the greenhouse.

Helesys wavered and put out a hand to catch herself. When her metal hand touched the black tower, she felt the building shake. She kept her hand on the stone, which felt like smooth glass, and waited.

The rumbling grew.

"Something is coming," she said.

The barbarian gripped his axe and the rogue slipped daggers from hidden sheaths. Helesys kindled her gauntlet.

Something descended down the black tower. The rumbling grew until Helesys's arm was rattling violently and she finally let go and backed away from the tower.

It stopped and then the tower split. Void-black gave way as twin doors slid open. Inside lay rich browns…

The inside was empty and completely bare. The floor and walls were made of wooden planks—as if they'd stepped into an unfurnished inn, except that the ceiling rose into an abyss. The floor was scuffed and scratched.

That wasn't right.

Helesys regarded the strange interior and then looked up to see the wooden walls extend upward past the limits of her vision.

"...It looks like a dumbwaiter," she finally said, the contraption coming back to her. "I think… Yes. We had them in my old house. You put food in and it travels up and down. Floor to floor."

Shawn peered in. "Huh. You might be right, lass."

"It will take us up. Out of the greenhouse," she added.

Taunauk grunted, hands still firmly clutching his battleaxe. "It is a killing chamber."

Both Helesys and Shawn turned. "What are you going on about?" Shawn asked.

"The doors will shut behind us. We will be trapped."

Helesys's first instinct was to reassure her comrade, but even though the elf had relaxed, her wand-arm had not.

Instead, she shrugged. "We have little choice."

~

Helesys, Taunauk and Shawn stepped out onto the wooden floor of the dumbwaiter, ready for violence.

The doors slid shut behind them. The glow of the greenhouse forgotten, the dim light of the dumbwaiter remaining. Again, she couldn't tell where the light came from—it was as if the light was in the very air itself.

For a moment, all Helesys could hear was her own breathing and the quiet hum of her gauntlet.

The floor shook gently beneath their feet, then began to rise. The walls slipped by as the floor took them up into the vertical abyss of the tower.

Dust floated around the chamber and grew, making several tiny whirlwinds around them. Surrounding them, the swirls grew and grew until their outlines became Terran.

Helesys, Taunauk and Shawn put their backs to one another and waited.

The whirlwinds coalesced into hollow men. They were ragged and wilting like that of a rotting corpse, but their skin was a single shade of grey-black, like a shadow given form. They had only the texture of rot, no color—no green rot or purple still-blood—there was only shadow. Their black teeth gnashed together. They staggered toward the group, silent in step and silent in breath except for their chattering mouths.

A moment later, the three adventurers lashed out with arcane blast, knife and axe, and the room was silent again. Helesys wand-arm had blown apart the upper half of one, shattering it into a black cloud. She watched the rest of it crumble to dust and fade away into the air.

Shawn mumbled, "Why does the barbarian have to be right?"

In the quiet of the moment, Helesys noticed something on the walls. Every few seconds, the dumbwaiter passed a gash in the wall—a pattern of five long slashes in the wood. Each grouping was nearly three feet long. As if made by a giant, clawed hand.

The air swirled again, coalescing into half a dozen hollow men. The three warriors again put their backs to one another and waited for the shades to form, then lashed out as soon as their black teeth began to chatter.

Helesys cut down two with rapid blasts from her gauntlet and then kept its power churning. Its power stoked her confidence. The room exploded into black mist again as Taunauk and Shawn cut down their shades shortly after.

Meanwhile, the great gouges in the walls grew more numerous.

Shawn said, "Um, guys… What are those on the wall?"

The barbarian groaned, "They are you, giving breath to fate."

"It is a test," Helesys said. "And it is going to get worse. Be ready. Look!"

The black mist swirled again, this time in only one place. A single shade.

The mist formed a skull, smooth and without the jagged, shadow-rot of the others. It peered at the adventurers with hollow eye sockets. It had no bottom jaw and its black tongue hung flaccid from its mouth. The mist swirled to form a body, building from the shoulders down. Its skin was smooth and thin, showing nobby bone and wiry muscles beneath.

"Get behind me," Taunauk said and stepped forward with Everfall and axe at the ready.

Helesys did not need to be told twice, for her wand-arm burned not just with power, but with a warning. She kept it leveled at the beast.

As the mist built from the shoulders down, the shade was transformed into something terrible. Its head and shoulders rose upward. The mist built it a long and lithe torso and its arms were the same. Helesys watched with terrible awe until the creature reached its full bearing. It had to have been twelve feet tall—nearly twice her height. It towered over all of them, even Taunauk.

The black mist built downward, finishing the bony and thin, sexless body. But the arms were all wrong. The black mist kept building the upper arms and did not stop at the shade's waist as normal arms would have. The upper arm ended at the hips and the forearms tapered down past its knees.

Its nobby feet were made before the hands were finished. Its hands seemed to blossom from thin wrists to enormous thin-spindled flowers. Its giant knuckles touched the floor. Its fingers were folded behind it and rose up from the floor, nearly three feet long—thin as spear-tips.

Helesys could not help but see the faint gouges on the floor anew. She no longer had to guess what creature made them.

Meanwhile, the weaver and the rogue were backing away. Taunauk was crouching behind Everfall.

The shade crouched, shrinking from its full, towering height to nearly looking Taunauk and Helesys in the eyes. The movement was slow enough not to be startling, except for the creaking joints and snapping tendons as the shade settled. Its enormously long limbs were now bent so much that its elbows were pointing upward like a bat walking on the ground.

Then the shade leveled its spear-tipped fingers at Taunauk and waved them. It was unnerving, for the gesture both reminded Helesys of two things: A parent teasing a child and of snakes wavering before they struck.

Helesys wasn't content to wait. She built the power in the gauntlet and fired, purple lightning churning from the embedded wand and through her palm. The blast rocketed in a silent scream toward the creature.

And it began to dance—a terrible, nightmarish ballet. The snaps and creaks of its body kept time.

Its long body contorted, arm and torso twisted to avoid the blast. The purple energy tore past it and exploded harmlessly against the passing wall of the dumbwaiter.

The shade raked its taunting fingers against Taunauk's shield. Its other arm extended across the room, reaching all the way to Helesys—fingers spread so they looked like five spear points. She fired again and again, but the lithe arm snaked around the blasts.

Helesys dove out of the way as the fingers sliced against the back wall, making a horrid scraping sound as they did. Then the hand retreated like a serpent recoiling.

Taunauk was spinning in a whirl of Everfall and axe, fighting against the five fingers of the shade's other hand. He did not see the other hand descending upon him.

"Look out!" Helesys shouted.

But Shawn leapt over the recoiling arm and sliced at it with silver, broadheaded dagger. The dancer didn't so much as groan or cry out, it merely waved the giant hand in the rogue's direction, the blades diverting from the barbarian and to him.

Helesys fired again and again, a dozen rapid blasts, but the cursed dancer contorted around them all.

"Shoot her!" Shawn shouted. In spite of the fray, there was laughter in his voice.

"I'm trying, you ass."

Then the black mist began to swirl again. The minor shades returned to the dumbwaiter, born again from the surrounding air. Slow and easy to hit. The elf weaver destroyed them as fast as they spawned, leaving Taunauk and Shawn to combat the dancer.

Helesys said, "If you have any tricks, rogue, now would be the time for them."

It wasn't Shawn that replied, but Taunauk. The whirling barbarian began to glow as if he'd been dipped in gold. Quiet orange flames flickered off him and trailed off his weapons. His whirl of strikes and guards became a blur, and he pushed forward against the twisted shade.

For once in the battle, the shade ceased reaching out to Shawn and Helesys, and fought against the barbarian alone.

"That's more like it," Shawn said.

"Focus on the little ones," she told the rogue. "I'll help Taunauk."

Shawn ran around the room, his cloak trailing through the air as he did. He became a flash of death, not unlike the dancer, slipping effortlessly between the grasps of shades and slicing through their necks with his white-bladed dagger, leaving them a dissolving cloud.

But with every shade struck down, another formed.

The dancer was backing away from Taunauk now and every time it tried to slip around him, the barbarian met it with ferocity.

Helesys churned her gauntlet and fired repeatedly. She no longer worried about hitting it, but about boxing it in so it could not escape—keeping the twisting beast within the reach of Taunauk's axe. Her blasts exploded against the walls, silhouetting the battle between the creature and the flaming barbarian. And theirs was a terrible dance of violence.

The stabbing of dagger fingers against ironwood and clanking of axe against bone grew loud over the fray. Even with his newfound speed, Taunauk could not press through the dancer's defenses, for each finger was a spear-tip, and it was as if he was fighting not one creature, but ten—all working in unison.

So Helesys switched tactics again. If the dancer would not be contained, the weaver would slow it. "*Lente et gravis*," she commanded.

The snaps and cracks of its limbs slowed, but only slightly. The beast barely seemed phased by the spell.

Deep in her arm, she felt the burning of the magekiller token. The bloodstained coin that would let her cut more easily through an enemy weaver...

The gangly creature was warded against magic—somehow the coin, or maybe her embedded wand, told her this. The creature would weather minor magic as easily as it evaded her arcane blasts. Zhug had warned her that the magekiller token wouldn't work against all magic things.

"You sneaky…" Helesys mumbled. "So that's why my blasts can't hit you. *Fine.*"

Helesys churned the power of her wand, compounding it to something that would be quite painful for her—had she used it as a blast. Instead, the weaver thought of Matron Mildé, the wolf-mother.

"Restu senmova, saltator."

The beast froze, its towering contorted body held fast by Helesys's magic. The horrid snaps and cracks of creaking tendons that had filled the room like music were paused, leaving nothing but footsteps and…

Ever so faintly, Helesys heard the snapping and creaking of bones and tendons—the sound of the dancer. But the sound came from somewhere behind her. Somewhere impossibly far away, from beyond the walls of the tower.

The weaver realized that the faint creaking she heard was not coming from somewhere in real space, but in mindspace. As she held the dancer with magic, their minds were linked.

And from that distant space, the sound of snapping grew louder. Pounding limbs on wood. The sound of the creature running toward her on all four limbs, body twisting and lumbering on gargoyle strides. She knew not whether it meant to pounce on her or worse—

"Taunauk, kill it!" she shouted.

But the glowing barbarian was already hacking the beast to pieces. He cleaved through its hands and then its knees. Meanwhile Shawn moved in a blur around the room, a flash of white dagger and cloak and death. Time seemed to slow and hang.

Still, the dancer charged through Helesys's mind—close now. Only seconds away.

Taunauk was hacking its hips and torso.

The lumbering grew terrible behind her and she flinched, fearing the beast would collide with her and break the spell.

The sound stopped. Meanwhile, the barbarian was not done—had not finished off the dancer.

Helesys blinked and the beast was in front of her, its massive body crouched so that it was face to face with her. Staring at her with empty eyes and drooping tongue.

The magekiller token burned hot in Helesys's gauntlet. It felt like a hot coal had been shoved inside her skin. It was not lost on the weaver that for the first time her metal arm felt the sensation of pain.

It was then that she felt the dancer's own mind. It might have only been a moment, but the moment stretched on and became a minute.

It was blank and empty. Yet something was there… small and horrid. Grotesque. It was like staring into pitch-black darkness and knowing that something was out there. Childlike terror welled up inside Helesys, yet it was as distant and as quiet as the dancer had been.

Helesys knew then that something was different about her. Somehow she was weathering the mind of the creature when she should not be able to—a normal mage would have succumbed to fear and broken the spell. It was not the fire of the magekiller token in her arm, nor the quiet terror that told her she was different…

In the quiet of the moment… Before Taunauk cut off the head of the dancer…

Helesys saw her own face reflected in the dancer as if she was looking in a mirror.

Then the beast vanished from sight.

~

Taunauk stood over the body of the creature. The chopped pieces turned to black mist and the barbarian's golden glow faded like a smoldering fire. His cloak was torn across the shoulder. The ironwood shield was covered in faint gashes. Whatever the dancer *had been*, it was no mere creature—for nothing so far had ever left a mark on Everfall.

Shawn cut through the last shade and its body burst into mist. He paused, daggers in hand and waited for more shades that never came. He was breathing deep and fast, sweat beading on his forehead.

"Is that it?" he whispered.

Taunauk grunted in protest. *Do not give breath to fate.*

The three shared a look of reservation. A moment later the dumbwaiter rumbled to a stop.

Helesys knelt in the dim light of the chamber. Legs and limbs weary from the magic effort. Her mind doubly so.

Shawn was kneeling beside her a moment later. "Are you alright?"

She nodded. "There is always recoil. There is physical pushback from the arcane cannon and mental pushback from other spells. It will pass in a minute."

Taunauk met her eyes, studying her with an animal's sight and concern. Taunauk had felt the holding spell before. Matron Mildé—the wolf mother—had used it on both of them. He knew what it was like.

"She touched the mind of the creature," Taunauk said. "It is no mere magic and no mere feat, for the inner minds of some are more treacherous than the icy winds you succumbed to, rogue—"

"No more of it," Helesys said. "It was not pleasant, nor a thing I wish to dwell on."

Taunauk grunted and held her gaze.

"Do you not approve?" she asked.

"You did what was necessary."

"Then why do you stare?"

The barbarian turned to the walls of the dumbwaiter as if he was searching for the words. "It is no mere feat, especially when you would weather it so easily. You were not powerless at the claws of the wolf-mother when she cast the spell on us. *I was.* And I do not wish to know of the creature's mind you touched. I suspect it is simple to hold a man, but a beast… the more single-minded the creature, the more vicious."

Helesys stood, despite her weariness. She was desperate to be done with the conversation. "Think no more of it." She walked over to the doors of the dumbwaiter and stood impatiently.

Shawn said, "Well, I agree that it was most impressive. Also, someone has gone to great lengths to ward this place and dissuade someone from taking this very path.

"It's strange though," the rogue continued, "that these things are not impassable. There are no traps, no impassable sigils… It's almost as if they do not wish to keep *everyone* out."

~ ~ ~

The Ramparts

The doors opened and the three heroes crept out into the cool night air.

The world had blossomed around them, for they were standing on one of the roofs of the castle. Dark stones lined the walkway and extended out across the roof. An equally dark wall lined the walkway on either side, shoulder-height with embrasure cut-aways for archers. Helesys paused to think of what use this cursed place would have for archers, and decided it must have been some kind of relic.

The walkway stretched across the roof for some hundreds of feet, from the dumbwaiter to a black tower. Its ebony tip rising up somewhere into the night sky. Beyond that, faint starlight kindled above them—a lie.

Some lost bit of childhood bubbled up in Helesys's mind, reminding her that starlight should be a promise. A thing wishes were made on. There would be none of that here. Not in this place.

"Look," Taunauk said and pointed with his axe.

High in the ebony tower were lights. They had been so tiny and the tower's stone so dark that the weaver had mistaken them for starry sky.

"That is our calling," the barbarian added.

Shawn peered through one of the arrow cut-aways and over the edge—then quickly backed away.

"Not wise to look down if one is afraid of heights," Helesys said, trying to lighten the mood. Mostly hers.

"I am not afraid of heights… I am afraid of falling," the rogue corrected. "And I am not so keen on waking up again. Alone."

Helesys looked to Taunauk, but the barbarian was staring to the left, over the wall. Looking off into the distance. The weaver followed his gaze and her jaw dropped.

She saw the forest—the Wode—stretch out to the horizon. The great treetops nearly as high as the walkway on which they stood.

Beyond them the infinite wall reached up and up, higher than the roof, higher even than the surrounding towers.

"That's not possible," Helesys said. The wall had not looked nearly so tall when she climbed up it. "It's all wrong…" If anything, the castle should dwarf the wall.

"You've been there?" Shawn asked.

"I tried climbing it."

"It is a trick," the outlander mumbled. "Do not dwell on it."

"He's right," Shawn said. "I'm starting to think this place has a mind and a will of its own. Playing tricks on your eyes is just another tactic it will use… What about over there?" He pointed to the right.

Helesys looked out over the other side of the wall. Out there was a churning, boiling sea—a mix of deep blue and white caps that stretched to the horizon. In the sky above the waters, black clouds swirled and blotted out the stars. Further to the side, where the ocean met the land, was a bog of twisted trees. A haze of green mist hung over it.

The weaver searched for the end of the infinite wall but could not find it. It disappeared abruptly, somewhere behind the black tower. The trick of the eye or impossible geometry of their prison.

"Let's move on," she said. Confusion and frustration swirling within her.

"Aye," the rogue said.

~

Taunauk led them across the black stone walkway. All three were ready with weapons and they did not have to wait long.

A black shadow swept across the sky and blotted out the stars as it passed. Twice they heard the flap of titanic wings and steadied themselves against the blasts of air. Helesys saw the outline of wings and serpentine body, and felt small—like a rodent frozen by the sight of a predator's shadow. She thought of the gigantic hydra from the flooded temple, and feelings of awe and fear came back to her. For this beast seemed even bigger than the hydra. Then the shadow dove and disappeared below the walkway.

Shawn muttered, "Something so big shouldn't be able to fly."

Then the beast came up from below and soared straight up in a shocking display of power. Its wings stretched from end to end of the walkway. As it passed, Helesys saw the reptilian head, tucked limbs and trailing tail.

Dragon.

"Do not breathe when the flames are near, lest it scorch your lungs," Taunauk said. "It will stay airborne. It will not land unless it grows desperate."

"Or to finish us off," Shawn added.

The barbarian shrugged. "Yes."

The outlander and rogue looked to Helesys, concern written plainly across the faces. They were adept fighters against foes they could reach, but they had no ranged weapons. The weaver did not remember much, but she knew not to get into a firefight with a dragon.

Helesys looked across the walkway to the black tower and the door at its base. "Then let's not prolong this. Run for the tower."

The shadow descended from the sky and grew large against the night.

The weaver churned the power of her gauntlet and felt the pang of the magekiller token within it—a warning that this beast would be warded against her magic, just as the Dancer was. But the dragon would not slip her blasts.

She leveled her gauntlet and compounded its power to the point of pain and not to injury. Purple power tore through the air and splashed against the dragon, highlighting its scales and horns in terrible glory, but still it came inexorably.

The dragon opened its maw and fire exploded from it. The horrid, crackling sound of the fire mixed with the high-pitched scream of the beast. Impossibly hot, even before it reached them.

The three dove for cover against the corner of the wall.

She held her breath and buried her face in the sleeve of her elbow. The heat grew painful and the world grew bright, even with her eyes buried. She felt like her cloak and clothes were set ablaze, but then the moment passed.

The fire faded and the flight of the dragon brought a gust of wind and cool air with it.

"Run!" Taunauk shouted.

The three leapt up and sprinted across the stone, blackened cloaks flailing in the wind. The tops of the wall were scorched and still kindling remnants of dragonfire, but thankfully the stone would not burn for long.

The dragon was already circling around again.

Helesys reached into her pocket for the crystal ring. Its power was of frost and, with any luck, it could bolster her power against the serpent. She slipped the ring onto the index finger of her mundane hand and felt a stab of cold.

A chill ran through her body, and she felt it travel deep within her. It went through her bones, up her neck, through her chest and even down her metal arm. The chill seemed to spasm inside her, as if there were ropes running through her body and one by one they were being cinched taught with violent pulls.

This time, when the dragon breathed fire and they dove to the ground, Helesys did not feel pain when the fire scorched the surrounding air. She merely felt discomfort.

They were up and running a moment later and now halfway across the wall.

The dragon flew high above them in an arching path. This time it would rain fire down on them and the cover of the walkway would be meaningless. They would be burned alive, unless Helesys did something.

She would not be killed and sent wandering. Not so soon.

She raised her gauntlet again, compounding its arcane power to the point of pain. She held it fast with her mundane hand and felt the power of winter flow through it. This time when she released its power, frost swirled with it in a mix of purple and white.

The blasts washed over the dragon and this time it screeched in pain and without fire. The massive beast flapped its wings and spiraled as it descended toward them, trying to avoid the brunt of the blasts.

Jolts of recoil flared in her shoulder and chest, but the elf kept blasting—even as the dragon grew large against the night sky.

At the last moment, it opened its maw and roared with fire breath.

Words came to her with a whisper and Helesys echoed them in turn, "*Hieme murum.*"

The weaver felt the chill leave her body, as if a long thread extended all through her alongside nerves and vessels. Down her legs and arms and feet and fingertips. The sensation of the thread leaving was somewhere between it slithering out and it being ripped out through her ring finger. She grimaced and ducked beside her comrades.

The power of the ring enveloped them, the long spindles of magic reaching around them in a jagged frost pattern. Cocooning them.

Then came the fire and instead of feeling the heat against her skin, she felt it inside her—where the crystalline thread *had been*. She felt—she knew—that the dragonsfire was a terrible weapon, but against the magic of the crystalline ring it was reduced from deadly to painful. The weaver grit her teeth. She could deal with pain if it meant making it to the tower.

Shawn screamed like a madman beside them. Helesys tried to look, but the world was bathed in a white and orange light from the mix of magic and dragonsfire. She could barely open her eyes.

When the fire passed, she released the shield and again shivered as the spike of magic crawled back along her nerves.

Taunauk was already on his feet and ready to run.

Shawn was crouched and staring at her, madness lingering in his eyes. He pointed a finger at her. "Don't you *ever* do that again."

"What? Save your life?"

"You know what I mean, *sorceress*. That ring is... " He backed away and stood on shaky legs. "I will go to the door. I'd rather be burned alive." Shawn was off and running across the walkway.

"That little—"

"To task," Taunauk said. "There will be another time."

The two of them stood back to back and searched the night sky, but did not see the dragon anywhere.

Helesys said, "Something so big should not be able to disappear so easily."

"Agreed."

From across the way, Shawn shouted. "The blasted door is locked!"

Taunauk shouted back, "Can it be broken down?"

"Doubtful, my hulking friend! Buy me time. I'll pick it."

Flames exploded from beneath and exploded up the side of the wall like a wave bursting against the rocks. Helesys and Taunauk shrank from the flames and the heat. She felt the crystal ring pulse in anticipation, but Helesys flared her gauntlet instead—choosing the warmth of strength over the icy stab of the ring's power. It was enough to weather an indirect blast of dragonfire.

The dragon circled beneath the wall and harassed them with flames. Every time they leaned over the edge to search, they were met with empty tree tops or a blast of fire.

"Almost there!" Shawn shouted.

Fire burst against the wall again. But when the blast faded, they felt the wall rumble and found themselves face to face with the dragon in all its terrible glory. It perched with its hind claws gripping the wall, crunching stone beneath them—each big enough to snatch them up. It stood upright and towered over them, taller than Zhug and even taller than the hydra. Its wings beat gently, helping it balance, but even those gusts threatened to blow them over the wall.

Helesys stared at the dragon and it stared back, green eyes behind a snub nose. Its scales were a shimmering black and purple against the night sky.

A metallic clank echoed across the walkway, deafening against the relative silence. Shawn turned triumphantly.

"I got it! ...Oh shit."

The dragon turned and opened its mouth. Helesys leveled her gauntlet—too slow.

Fire erupted and roared across the roof, directly toward Shawn.

A swirl of ice and purple leapt from her wand-arm at the dragon's chest, and the beast screeched. It fell back, wounded, but swept the fireblast across the entire walkway.

Helesys and Taunauk ducked. She called on her wand-arm and the crystal ring to protect them. The resilience granted by her wand eased the pain of the crystal ring, but not the discomfort, and the weaver still grit her teeth against the sensation.

When the fire passed, the weaver and the barbarian ran as fast as they could to the door. Their cloaks were charred and fell off their backs as they ran. The stone was steaming and patchwork flames lingered. Helesys could feel the heat of the stone beneath the soles of her boots.

Somewhere below, they heard the beating of the dragon's wings.

"Shawn!" Taunauk called.

The rogue came running along the outer wall of the tower, half-climbing, half-running along the wall. When he got close to the walkway his steps grew awkward. "Ow. Ow. Hot. Ow." He landed clumsily next to them.

The door was wrought iron and glowing dark red from the heat of the dragonsfire. A procession of dozens of wolves adorned it.

Taunauk used the blade-tip of his axe to push on the steaming door handle, and then the three slipped inside the black tower.

The last thing they heard was the angry screech of the dragon.

~ ~ ~

The Wizard's Sanctum

They walked up the narrow spiral staircase, which wrapped around the outer wall of the tower and up to the right. The stone of the steps and walls was rough—lightly tread. Sconces lit by magic burned faintly on the inner wall to the left. Roughly every quarter turn of the stairs, they passed a window to the night sky. The glass was grimy and no stars shined through them, nor could they see the shadow of the dragon.

Taunauk went first, shield and axe in hand. Without his cloak, the barbarian seemed thinner in stature, but it was only because it hid the taper of his back. Muscles rippled beneath the sleeves of his tunic and even beneath the thick leather over his back and thighs. Flashes of memory came back to her, making her think of the great statues of the gods brought to life.

Meanwhile, Helesys had lost her own cloak too. She wore a similar leather vest, overtop a chainmail shirt and long tunic for the base layer. It was strange to feel bare without her cloak and so many layers remaining, but she did.

She kept her gauntlet half-raised and at the ready. More than once it caught her eye—no longer could she pretend her arms were the same when hidden beneath the cover of her cloak. Even beneath chainmail, the hard curves of the metal gauntlet were apparent.

Helesys kindled her wand to bolster her resolve. Not for strength or to dull the pain, but to stomach the stench of burnt cloth and burnt hair that lingered on the staircase.

"What do you think is up there?" Shawn whispered. Of the three of them, he looked completely unscathed and had kept his cloak.

"Hopefully it will not be long until we find out," Helesys replied.

"Keep your eyes open for traps," Taunauk said. "Doubtful the passage is unguarded."

They climbed the last two revolutions of the stairs in un-easy, unperturbed silence and came to a single wooden door at the top of the stairs. Bare redwood except for the metal wolf's head in the center—a knocker.

The three exchanged a glance before Taunauk wearily rapped with the metal knocker.

A man's equally weary voice called from inside, "You may enter."

Taunauk carefully pushed the door open with Everfall and led them inside.

~

The room inside the tower was massive and brightly lit. It must have been over fifty feet across and nearly as high—easily bigger than the simple tower it appeared from the outside.

The first level was littered with workbenches, reams of metal and glass and stone. Along the wall were dozens of chests and above those hung all manner of hammers and pliers and tools. A massive stone forge lay in the center, glowing red hot. Helesys understood that it drew heat from somewhere deep below and through the center of the tower. How she knew this, she could not say.

Half-a-dozen creatures worked at the tables, hammering and crafting away. They were thin and long-limbed. Their skin was a mix of pale flesh and dark green scales. Some more mottled than the rest. Their eyes were another mix: Puss-yellow while some were so dark they seemed sunken inside the sockets.

None of the creatures paid the adventurers any mind.

So Helesys searched the rest of the room and upward.

Tall, colorful stained glass windows covered most of the walls. Depictions of wolves adorned many of them. Wars, strange machines, and ancient runes adorned others. There was another floor above them with stairs wrapping around the edge of the room.

It occurred to Helesys that she couldn't remember seeing windows when they were outside the tower.

"Be careful," she said. "We are in another sorcerer's dwelling."

"I am nothing of the sort," called the man from upstairs. "Come up and see for yourselves."

The adventurers walked up the narrow stairs to the next level, while keeping a watchful eye on the creatures below.

At the top, they came to the final level. The room towered above them in a daunting open foyer, ending at the pointed roof and supporting trusses. Long flowering vines hung down from the trusses, creating a miniature hanging garden above their heads.

Bookshelves lined the spaces between the windows and reached up past the vines. The floor was littered with dozens of pedestals adorned with sculptures and workbenches covered in parchment, beakers and wands.

And in the center of it all, stood the man—the voice they had heard. His face was lined with wrinkles, his eyebrows and beard completely white, the latter of which hung down to the sash around his waist. His robes were a brilliant white and crimson and trimmed in golden braids. The hood was pulled forward, hiding the rest of the wizard's brow and eyes. He stood with arms crossed, hands hidden beneath his sleeves.

The old man glanced up, then pulled back his hood, revealing a length of braided hair in the same beautiful white. In spite of his age, he stood tall and was broad chested beneath his robe.

"My name is Amadeus Mordan. I've gone by many names over the years but that is the one you may know me by."

"Taunauk Aonar."

"Helesys of House Byyra."

"Shawn." The rogue glanced sideways at Helesys, betraying false confidence.

Amadeus raised an eyebrow at the three of them. "I see you carry Everfall. That means several things: You have met with Zhug, he has found you worthy of calling you an ally, and gifted you with treasure. Not only that, but you have brought that treasure with you across death and to another realm. *That* is a power that very few can claim."

A leather-bound tome from high on the shelves fell and then glided over to the mage with the grace of a bird. It stopped and hovered open beside him. A pen flew out of his pocket and began to scribble notes in the book without Amadeus having so much as whispered.

Helesys smiled. "How did you do that?"

"Young lady, of all the wondrous things in my sanctum, a quill-writing spell is what impresses you?"

"It's not the spell. It's that you did it without moving your hands or uttering incantations. I... I can make raw magic with my gauntlet, but I still must use words with most of my spells."

Amadeus smiled warmly. "I know. I watched you fight your way through my traps and my minions. That is a strange contraption." He pointed to her arm. "But then, most elven things are. They guard their magic close."

Helesys ignored the comment. "You were scrying on us?" She thought back to the barracks when Zhug had scryed on them. "I could feel Zhug watching us... Why couldn't I feel your presence?"

"Zhug is a powerful mage, but he has a heavy touch and a giant's subtlety. But to your first question, this is *my* sanctum and I have spent a hundred lifetimes warding it. It makes my stone men better able to resist your spells, for instance. There are a great many things I can do here that would not be possible elsewhere—casting without incantations is but one."

A great rush of wind sounded from outside and Helesys turned in time to see the black dragon's silhouette descend on the tower. The great beast was coming right for them, its shadow growing huge against the bright glass.

Or rather for a small opening in the glass. The tower rumbled as the dragon landed on the wall and then pushed its face toward the opening of the glass—which was no wider than a scroll of parchment.

The dragon's snout shrunk as it pushed through the opening. The head, then neck and body and wings and then tail— its size changing from gargantuan to that of a bat or a cat.

The shrunken dragon swirled and danced in the open air of the tower, spiraling up the vines through the rafters and back down to rest upon Amadeus's shoulder. It's shimmering black scales, a stark contrast to the mage's white robes.

"That being another one of them?" Shawn asked.

Amadeus nodded and smiled. "If Zhug trusts you, then I will trust you. And if you trust Shawn, then so shall I."

The old mage sat down and a chair materialized behind him. The back was two feet too high and it was covered in plush red fabric. He sighed when he sat down, as if finally relaxing enough to show his age.

Out of the corner of her eyes, Helesys saw the same tall chairs appear behind her comrades. One was behind her as well.

"Sit," Amadeus said, "and regale me with your stories and with your questions."

~

The three sat tentatively and faced the old mage. Helesys focused on her wand-arm, but felt no stirring or warning of danger. She sat in the soft chair and, for a moment, closed her eyes in comfort as her sore shoulders sank into the soft backing.

Taunauk leaned Everfall against the left side of the chair and sat with his battleaxe across the arms of the chair, his hands resting on the hilt. The seat expanded, wood creaking, to accommodate the width of him. In spite of his resignation, she noticed him lean back and the great muscles of his arms slacken.

Shawn had been the first to sit. Now he slouched in the chair, legs crossed. Hanging foot bouncing.

Amadeus sat across from them. The shrunken dragon lay curled on his lap—far from the giant terror of the sky that it had been only minutes ago. He stroked its back idly. The leather-bound book and pen sat on a small wood table to his right—another thing he had conjured from the air.

Helesys spoke for her and Taunauk. She told the mage of their journey through the flooded temple, of the fishmen and the hydra; the battle with Zhug's goblins and narrow escape from the many hands of Shomosk; wandering through the forest, the tribe of wolf-men and the Deacon's village, and her ill-fated climb up the infinite wall; the buried hive and the hiding glassmen.

Amadeus listened intently. Twitches of emotion flashed across his face, as if he had seen and felt much of what they did.

Helesys spoke casually about their journey, not meaning to elaborate as she did, but she couldn't help but feel comforted by Amadeus's demeanor. As if he truly did want to hear about their journey.

And so, when she got to the greenhouse, she trailed off. "You already know the rest. "We fought our way to your sanctum."

"Yeah," Shawn said, "What was with that creepy thing in the dumbwaiter? And all that stuff in the basement?"

"It was a test," Amadeus said, glancing at Helesys. "Do you think a man of my stature has the time to speak with every fool who wanders into his realm?"

"Are there many fools who wander here?" Helesys asked.

"More than just you. Do you recall the scorched hills and frost? But then I was a fool once."

Taunauk spoke, "How long have you been here, good weaver?"

Amadeus wrinkled his brow in thought. Then the tome on the end table rose and changed—its back flashed from brown leather to blue satin—and opened for him.

"That's what I thought. Some thousand years more or less; more than a two dozen lifetimes. Long enough to see the castle evolve... remake itself anew. The only things I know for certain are that I've seen two sunrises and I'm reaching the limits of my magic."

Helesys glanced at her comrades and found them already looking to her.

"I do not know which questions to ask," Taunauk said. "You know more of magic than I."

Amadeus chuckled and corrected him, "This place is no mere magic."

"Then it is magic by another name," the barbarian replied. "It is only wondrous because you do not know the spell."

The old mage held out a hand and a green egg floated over to him from a pedestal in the back of the room—one of the many sculptures and things on display. It was nearly two feet tall, but in spite of its size, Amadeus handled it with ease. It was a green and white jade that sparkled and nearly seemed to *flow*, as if it was not rock but a crystalline liquid. Patches and swirls of color ebbed like storm clouds, and each touch of the wizard sent ripples across the surface.

"Do you have any idea what this is?" the mage asked, holding the egg up for them. Three heads shook. "It is a *soul trap*. A bottled world. It can be anything from a house to a city to a continent. An old mage can live many more lifetimes within its borders. Soon it will be my escape—inward instead of outward."

"So, which is it?" Shawn asked. "City? House?"

Amadeus glared at the rogue a moment. "It is a fond memory—a personal memory. What is inside is not important." The old mage sighed and let the jade egg float in the air beside him. "Have you noticed any great rules of the castle?"

Taunauk spoke, "Things die, but are reborn elsewhere."

Shawn said, "Most people cannot bring things back when they die. Except us." He gestured to the three of them.

Helesys eyed the rogue, noting that he too had that ability. But she had other concerns.

"But things do die here," she said. "Eventually things are ground away. The Deacon spoke of a whole civilization before the fishmen that was forgotten. The Deacon feared for himself… You fear for yourself."

Amadeus nodded. "Gods help me, I do."

She continued, "Nothing is born here. The only new things are made-things."

The old mage nodded, "You have seen many made-things, though you might not have realized. My workers, the treasure horde of mimicry, my stone men and drakes. The dancer in the tower. My dragon, Iogo. Pitiful Lull, you called him—an unfortunate mishap. Many of the Deacon's villagers—"

"But that's not important," Helesys interrupted. "If things are ground to dust here and none new can be born… That is why the dungeon continues to capture new beings." She glanced at the green egg. "This place is a soul trap. Souls are drawn in and live in a bottled world."

Amadeus nodded, a bittersweet smile on his lips.

~

Where the mage's sanctum had felt warm and filled with light, it now felt clouded and cold with the realization about the dungeon. Helesys looked to the jade egg that floated beside the old mage. To think that the egg and the dungeon were one and the same…

Except that it was not so parallel. Amadeus had spent a significant amount of time on the egg; on his escape—his *alone*. So the egg was limited. The dungeon was not. Within its confines, there were gods and whole civilizations trapped. Uncountable more than Amadeus's small relic could hold.

"So... how do we escape?" Shawn asked.

"We are seeking the Wolf-Knight and the Gatekeeper," Helesys said, "but we don't know where they are."

"You are on the right path, then," Amadeus replied. The shrunken dragon, Iogo, stretched on his lap and curled up again.

"What?" Shawn asked. "Are they some kind of dungeon masters?"

Amadeus smiled and waved away the question. "Nothing so crass as that."

"Why don't you seek them?" Taunauk asked Amadeus. "You are powerful."

The old mage shrugged. "Much of my power is imbued here." Amadeus looked fondly on the jade egg. He waved a dismissive hand and sent the egg floating back to its pedestal across the room. "It would be too great a risk to die by the King's hand and be sent wandering without my relics; to have little hope of returning here. When I was young… But to do so now would be the worst kind of folly.

"Besides, the Wolf-King is far beyond even my power. He has relics that would shame even Zhug and his throne room is steeped in magic that shames my sanctum. Were you to confront him, you would be fighting in *his throne room*. He will conjure wonders and horrors that I cannot fathom. Lost magics and hellish curses… In a world of trapped gods, the Wolf-King reigns. You must expect anything and everything."

"What of the Gatekeeper?" Helesys asked.

And as she uttered the words, a chill ran down her spine, sudden and deathly cold—Helesys felt as if ice-water had been poured on her.

Taunauk rose and scanned the room and was followed quickly by Shawn and Helesys. Weapons drawn.

"You felt that too?" Helesys asked and Taunauk grumbled.

Amadeus twitched and shook his head quickly, "Do not speak of *her*."

While her comrades watched the room, Helesys turned toward the old mage. Amadeus was gripping the arms of his chair so fiercely his nails punctured the fabric, revealing white cotton beneath. His head shook back and forth in a steady metronome.

"No. No. No. I cannot." His voice strained, groaned, cracked, "*He* is listening."

Helesys heard the whisper crawl in her ear—the same that haunted her at the infinite wall.

Answers you have gained by sacrifice are not yours to give freely.

"What was that?" Shawn asked.

Iogo startled from the mage's lap. It fluttered away, past the hanging vines to the safety of the trusses high in the foyer.

"Nothing good," Helesys said.

"Run, you fools!" Amadeus groaned. "I cannot—"

The old mage's eyes turned black, clouded by possession magic. His body shook violently, as if his body were being moved against its will.

From below came a clanking of metal and a breaking of glass. The gangly workers snarled, and then the stairs shook with steps as they ran up. Hammers and pokers in hand.

"Keep them at bay," Helesys said. She turned to the conflicted Amadeus. "*Restu sonmuvo, maljuna mago.*"

Taunauk and Shawn circled around her, Everfall, axe and knives clanging against craftsman's tools. But this was distant to the weaver.

Her mind became locked with Amadeus's. Her heart raced, thinking of her last battle of wills with the dancer. How the monster's mind had become an image on top of the real world. How the monster had been both terrifying and a reflection of some deep part of her.

But this time the mage's sanctum grew dim and filled with silvery mist. Somewhere high above, blackness loomed. A starless night sky.

She still heard the clangs and clashes of her comrades, but they had vanished. Reduced to specters somewhere in the mist.

Amadeus was in front of her, clutching the arms of his red chair. Eyes black and body convulsing.

And as she stared at the struggling mage, she felt his mind and his body. Her joints ached with age and a dozen lifetimes of toil and use. Yet she felt strong—stronger than she had ever been when calling upon her wand—the same dozen lifetimes of wear had brought untold knowledge. Magic smoldered through the old mage's body, keeping him not just alive but youthful.

The mix of strength and weariness was heavy on her shoulders. As if she might fall asleep at any moment—kept awake only by tea and endless walking. An old mage staying alive for one more day, one more morning. Toiling over work that would never truly be finished. One more day before he finally escaped to his jade dream.

Amadeus stood and Helesys's eyes grew wide.

Somewhere in the gloom, she heard Shawn's faint shout muted to a whisper, "Helesys, It's not working!"

Amadeus was no longer shaking, yet she could still feel something… large hands on her shoulders—his shoulders.

Standing behind the white and crimson robed mage was another. The figure's shoulders loomed above Amadeus, and it made the old mage look like a child in stature. *The Wolf-King.* The mage—the god—wore deep blue robes that seemed to glisten with power. Their face was covered by a white wolf mask, one simple in design yet shone brilliantly.

And behind the Wolf-King loomed darkness—the dungeon. Black as a starless night. It rose up above the mist and into oblivion, and Helesys nearly fell backward to follow it.

"Run," the old mage whispered, the slightest twitch beside his lips. She could still feel him fighting the control of the Wolf-King.

"Blast the window. Jump. It is the only way. Do it before —"

The Wolf-King lunged for her. Reaching a hand nearly clear across the room.

Helesys startled and broke the spell. The mist and the Wolf-King disappeared. The sanctum reappeared, as did Taunauk and Shawn. The two warriors stood over the slain bodies of the gnarled workers. Ash and dust covered the floor, piled in places where blood should have pooled.

Shawn said, "I take it your trump card didn't work?"

"No," Helesys replied. She turned to the old mage. "We don't wish to fight you."

But Amadeus was far away or buried beneath the will of the Wolf-King. His eyes black. His muscles spasmed quietly as the fight left the mage.

Helesys whispered, "Amadeus told us to blast the window and jump."

Shawn said, "but that's suicide."

"Falling's not so bad."

Taunauk growled, "We are running out of time. Blast the window."

Before Helesys could turn, the entire tower rumbled.

Helesys fought to stay on her feet. There were clangs and smashes as tools and projects fell and broke on the floor—the jade egg hovered peacefully above the table. Amadeus stared at them, eerily still on his feet.

The shelves rattled and books fell off the shelves and then levitated in the air. The tomes opened, filling the air with hisses and crackles as hundreds of beams of magic rained down from them like a dam burst. Rays of frost, fire, purple, jade, and a dozen colors in between scorched the hanging vines and the floor in front of the shelves and turned, arching and sizzling across the wizard's sanctum toward the trio.

Beams carved around Amadeus, the old mage frozen in his own inner battle of wills.

The dragon flew down from the rafters, screeching, and the trio cowered—ready to leap away from its flames—but the dragon breathed fire toward its master instead. The flames curled and wrapped around Amadeus, as if he were protected by some invisible barrier. Still, he stayed frozen—his shaking was so faint, Helesys feared all the fight had gone out of him.

Helesys turned for the window and blasted it with her gauntlet. The silent scream of purple gave way to shattering glass and rushing wind. The magic light that lit the windows was no more and the bleak night shown beyond.

Then the beams flicked toward them.

Taunauk shouted, ""*Foghar siorruidh.* Get behind me!" A protective veil of autumn leaves burst forth from Everfall, swirling and dancing with hurricane speed.

Rather than try to counter the power of Amadeus's sanctum, Helesys turned her own magic toward the Wolf-King's hold on the mage. "*Dissolvere vincula.*" She bolstered her counterspell. Power hummed and built in her wand-arm and the gauntlet rattled in her shoulder.

At first, she feared it was feeble, but she *felt* Amadeus grow stronger, regaining his hold over his own faculties. His muscles shook with renewed struggle. The book beams swung wider in their arcs, their aim disturbed.

Still, some beams found their marks. They burned hot and cold, and smoked against the swirling autumn leaves. Jade beams seared through completely and scorched the ironwood of the shield itself.

The tiny dragon danced through the beams, accosting its master with fire. The fire twisted and swirled around Amadeus, never quite touching him.

Even with their combined might, they would wilt against Amadeus and the sanctum's magic.

And through it all, Helesys could feel the Wolf-King looming over the castle like a gargantuan specter. Somehow, the king was fighting all of them at once, even through the wards and spellguards of the sanctum.

"We must run!" Taunauk shouted.

"No," Shawn said through the maelstrom.

"Don't be a fool," she replied, straining to hold the counterspell.

"I'm not ready," the rogue said.

"Ready for what?" she asked.

"I'm not ready to wander alone again."

Helesys met the rogue's eyes and her heart wrenched in her chest. But she did not have more than a moment to pity him.

The Wolf-King broke her counterspell, and Helesys felt like an ice pick had been driven through her skull. She screamed and the rain of magic beams broke Everfall's veil of Autumn.

Chaos followed. The world went mute. Helesys thought of blastshells. Of rumbling and heat.

"Run!" came the barbarian's muffled shout amidst the fervor.

Fear gripped her and Helesys followed without thinking. The barbarian and the weaver leapt out of the tower. Out into the cool night sky.

She turned in midair to see Shawn running toward Amadeus. He looked impossibly small against the magic onslaught, as if he alone was standing against an army.

Then he was gone from sight as Helesys and Taunauk plummeted down the side of the castle. As they fell, the void-black stones seemed to rise up and up as if the castle—the dungeon—was growing and going to swallow the stars.

The wind grew to a roar and Helesys again felt the presence of the Wolf-King, head thrown back in a laugh, in a sneer. Instead of slamming into the ground, she feared she would fall into the maw of the beast.

Then the sky exploded in orange fire. Some catastrophic spell had blown out all the windows of the tower and fire bloomed in the night. A little black dot was thrown out into the night—Shawn. He had fared no better.

Then there was blackness. Silence.
But this time there was no peace.

~ ~ ~

The floor appeared beneath her. Helesys landed and tucked into a roll.

The barbarian landed beside her, catching himself with strength.

But the two were alone in that cursed room; Shawn was nowhere to be found.

The weaver felt a pang of loss. She knelt on the stone and bowed her head. "Movernus, guide him."

"He knew," Taunauk said. The barbarian was already walking off toward the wall of sconces.

Helesys paused a moment, for she looked upon her comrade's cloak and then her own. The cloth restored completely and upon their backs again. Renewed as their bodies were.

The elf rose from her knee. "Knowing does not make the task any easier. It does not make coming back alone any easier."

Taunauk grunted in agreement, then pulled a sconce from the wall. Chips of stone scattered across the floor.

Did Shawn wake up in a room like this? Was he waiting for them? Or was he like Taunauk, already pushing forward? Why did the ring of frost pain him so?

Helesys felt the same kinship with the rogue that she felt with Taunauk—that they knew one another in their lives outside the dungeon. So why were she and Taunauk reborn together when Shawn was born alone?

She cursed the questions swirling in her head and fought back the lump in her throat.

Helesys said, "We have a more pressing matter: What of the Wolf-King?"

The barbarian paused. "We have avoided his gaze until now. Do you feel his presence still?"

"No. But that does not change the fact that he possessed Amadeus in *his own sanctum*. That is no mere feat to break through so many wards and imbued spells, nor to fight the will of Amadeus and fight us at the same time. The Wolf-King is no mere mage or conjurer."

Taunauk shrugged. "One does not become king of a place like this without merit."

Helesys thought of Amadeus's last words to them… She had asked about the Gatekeeper. "Do… Do you think the Wolf-King holds her prisoner? What even is she?"

"Impossible questions," the barbarian grumbled. "It is no matter. We will gather the strength to meet him. That is our boon."

Helesys shook her head, then looked at the ring of frost. Even now, without using it, she could feel the chill grip around her finger. She remembered the thin, painful tendrils of connection when she called upon it.

"Or it is our curse," she said. "What do you feel when you use Everfall?"

Taunauk glanced to the shield upon his back and pulled it overhead. He ran a hand over the surface with care. "I feel a connection. The roots and leaves I call upon feel like fingernails in the dirt or hair caught in the wind. I feel strength as weapons crash upon it. Most weapons…"

The outlander turned the shield so she could see the front. A black gash cut across the face of the ironwood where one of the magic beams had both cut and scorched it simultaneously. It was a shallow gash… Yet it was a mar nonetheless; a mar that had not been repaired. Everfall had been marred by the dancer in the dumbwaiter, but those scratches were no more.

Taunauk's face soured. "What does this mean?"

Helesys walked over and ran her metal-hand over the shield, hoping that she might feel something. Something to make sense of it.

She felt nothing. The weaver shook her head. "It means in this world of death and rebirth, there are things that can maim… and lingering deaths that can break the cycle completely."

Taunauk hoisted the shield upon his back again—as if he couldn't look upon it further.

Helesys went on. "Items imbued with magic are different from mundane ones, like our cloaks and packs. They have memories, of a sort. Perhaps that is why they can be marred. It is similar to our bodies being made whole, but our minds remembering the dangers and horrors... Our minds are marred."

She looked at her metal hand, taking in the sight of the blue-tinted metal. She shuddered at the thought of her own arm becoming marred like Everfall—the fact that she might lose its use completely. A puzzling fact, because she had already lost the mundane arm once—one more event that she could not recall.

"It changes nothing," Helesys finally said. "Though we do not fear death, and we are weary of pain and loss... We will escape."

Taunauk nodded, half-smiling in the gloom. "We will grow stronger. Yes. We will escape."

The barbarian turned and led the way with torch in hand. The weaver followed.

When they got to the hallway entrance, Helesys turned and looked back on that cavernous room—the room they always returned to—hoping to see Shawn again. Hoping in vain that he would be spared from wandering alone.

"We will see him again," Taunauk said.

Helesys felt this to be true, but gave voice to doubt instead. "How can you be sure?"

"I feel it to be true. He echoes with me, as do you."

The weaver smiled and followed Taunauk down the stone hallway. It was a good enough answer to an impossible question.

~ ~ ~ ~ ~

<u>From the Author</u>: Don't worry. Shawn will be appearing again alongside Helesys and Taunauk again in the main series. But in the meantime, he'll be getting his own recurring short stories!

If you want to read about Shawn's encounters below the wizard's tower, sign up for my Monthly Newsletter at <u>SamuelFlemingBooks.com</u> and you'll get a free short story featuring Shawn. New shorts with the lovable rogue will be coming every two months or so, and delivered right to your Email.

If you like the cover art, you can also get Free Phone and Desktop Backgrounds featuring art from *A Battleaxe and a Metal Arm*!

By signing up, you'll also be the first to hear about publishing news and sales alerts.

Don't like spam? Me neither. You'll get 2-3 Emails at first, all containing the above-mentioned free stuff. After that, expect 1-2 Emails a month.

~ ~ ~

NEXT TIME ON
*A BATTLEAXE AND
A METAL ARM*
Book 6:

*The Cannibal
Dining Room*
Available September 2021

Spoiler–Free excerpt from *BAMA 6*

They were getting toward the end. Fog rolled into the hallway, rolling past their shins and not quite covering the stone. They walked deeper and deeper into it and soon could not see more than a few hundred feet in front or behind them. Eventually the cool mist clung to Helesys's face and hair.

Taunauk walked with Everfall shield and torch in hand. Helesys kindled her wand-arm, if only for reassurance. The two walked in uneasy silence.

Miles later, the hallway ended.

Beyond was a jungle. Green ferns and stalks pierced the veil between the gray light of mist and dusk. Underbrush and dead leaves crackled beneath their feet. The chirps and squawks of birds filtered through the mist.

Taunauk grunted in dissatisfaction and stepped cautiously into the gloom.

"What's the matter?" Helesys asked, following.

"Mist."

When the barbarian didn't elaborate further, she prodded. "What's wrong with it, other than not being able to see danger clearly?"

"It's cold and wet. It gets everywhere. *And* you can't see danger clearly."

Helesys smirked, the humor a small release of tension. "Do you think the hallway…"

The elf turned and saw that the stones that marked the hallway were already gone. It had only been a few steps away. Now it was nothing more than empty air. She walked back and ran her metal hand over where the entrance *should be*, but found nothing. No hidden stones, no remnant of magic. Nothing but mist.

She said, "I'm beginning to think that is a trick of the dungeon or the Wolf-King, and that they don't like us retracing our steps."

"They are herding us." Taunauk said the words matter-of-factly. He cast the torch aside, no longer needing it in the perpetual gray light and drew his giant battleaxe.

"Herding us to where? To what end?"

"To death—the same end we always meet." He turned and studied his comrade. "Does that trouble you?"

Helesys met his eyes. "No. The act doesn't bother me. The reasoning behind it gives me pause."

"You assume there is reason behind it. Most creatures do not act on reason. Most Terrans don't either."

They shared a gallows' smirk. Helesys said, "On that we can agree."

To be continued September 2021

Thank you for Reading

I hope you enjoyed reading this story as much as I enjoyed writing it.

If you did, I would massively appreciate a short review on Amazon or your favorite book website. Reviews are crucial for any author, and a starred review or even just a line or two can make a huge difference.

It's especially true for the start of a series. Thanks and I hope you enjoy the next one!

Looking for more Bite–Sized Fantasy?

You might like **Tales from Another World, Volume 1**. The first installment contains stories about an undead sorcerer, a druid grove under attack, strange mermaids, a possessed church, a witch sentenced to burn, and commoners caught in-between.

The 2nd installment is out now!

What questions do you have about *A Battleaxe and a Metal Arm*?

If you've read this far, hopefully you'll read a bit further—both in this book and across the series. I'm not sure how most authors write serials and how much of it is flying by the seat of their pants, but that's not how I do things. For all the major questions that might come up in BAMA, I already have answers for 95% of them. Same goes for the major plot points, twists and climaxes. That might sound boring to some, especially some of you other authors who enjoy variations of writing into the dark, but I think having a solid blueprint is paramount to writing a long series.

So, what questions do you have about the story? Here are a few:

1) ~~What is the dungeon?~~ It's a soul trap of overwhelming size and power. But where did it come from? Is it a force of nature or an ill-made weapon, or perhaps something else entirely?

2) Who were Helesys and Taunauk before they got trapped? At this point, we know little more than their names and abilities. How well did they know each other beforehand?

3) How did Helesys get her metal arm?

4) Who is Shawn? Why does he feel so familiar to Helesys and Taunauk?

5) Who is the Wolf King and what sinister plans does he have for our heroes? How did he come to rule over the Dungeon? How does the Gatekeeper factor into all this?

Did I miss any questions? Probably. Connect with me and other *BAMA* fans on social media and compare questions!

I've got plans. I've got answers. And I've got them on a drip-feed. Keep reading and expect to find out a little more to the mysteries with each installment. Hopefully, you're as excited about this series as I am.

Connect with the Author

If you want to stay up to date on the latest about Samuel's publishing news and blog, check out his website and consider signing up for his monthly newsletter.

www.SamuelFlemingBooks.com

Samuel can also be found on Reddit, Goodreads and Facebook.

Samuel Fleming is a Science Fiction and Fantasy author.

He grew up in Maryland, spending most of his time swimming and writing. Swimming gave him a lot of time to daydream, so the two hobbies complemented each other well. Idle day dreams turned into stories, some of which stuck with him for years. These days he swims a little less and writes a lot more.

He loves a good story no matter the medium: Books, TV, video games, comics, tabletop RPG's, or podcasts–most of which he attempts to share with his wife and three kids, and occasionally on his blog.